JUST A THUNDERSTORM

BY GINA AND MERCER MAYER

For Cameron Gurkin

A GOLDEN BOOK • NEW YORK

Just a Thunderstorm book, characters, text, and images © 1993 Mercer Mayer. LITTLE CRITTER, MERCER MAYER'S LITTLE CRITTER, and MERCER MAYER'S LITTLE CRITTER and Logo are registered trademarks of Orchard House Licensing Company. All rights reserved under International and Pan-American Copyright Conventions. Published in the United States by Golden Books, an imprint of Random House Children's Books, a division of Random House, Inc., New York, and simultaneously in Canada by Random House of Canada Limited, Toronto. Originally published in 1993 by Western Publishing Company, Inc. Golden Books, A Golden Book, and the G colophon are registered trademarks of Random House, Inc. Library of Congress Control Number: 2002096249

ISBN 0-375-82633-5

www.goldenbooks.com

Printed in the United States of America   First Random House Edition 2003

10 9 8 7 6 5 4 3

Mom said a thunderstorm was coming.
The sky was dark and the wind was blowing.

I helped Mom bring in the clothes
from the clothesline.
And my brother picked up our toys
from the yard.

Then we heard a faint rumbling noise.
But I wasn't scared. I knew it was just
a little thunder.

It started pouring down rain. Mom forgot to roll up the car window, so I went with my brother to do it for her.
We got soaked.

While Mom was making dinner,
we saw lightning.

Then the power went out.

Dad lit some candles and
made a fire in the fireplace.

We roasted marshmallows and hot dogs
for dinner. It was just like a real campout.

The power came back on just in time for our favorite TV show. But the weatherman kept interrupting it.

Then it really started thundering loud.

Soon Mom and Dad said it was time for bed.
But I didn't want to go to bed while there was
so much thunder.

Dad let me leave the light on so I could read.
But that didn't help. The thunder was too loud.

I tried listening to my favorite tape, but
I could still hear the thunder and see the lightning.

So I put my head under my pillow.
That didn't help, either.

I started crying and called Dad.

I said, "I hate thunderstorms."
Dad said, "Thunderstorms can seem scary,
but they're really very good. They bring rain
so that plants can grow and we can have
enough water to drink."

But I was still scared. So I climbed into bed
with my brother.

He said he wasn't scared. Then there was a big clap of thunder. We both screamed. That scared us even more.

We ran into Mom and Dad's room. They said we could sleep on their floor.

The next morning when I woke up
the sun was shining.

Mom said, "See, thunderstorms are nothing to be afraid of."

I didn't say anything. I just went outside
to play with my brother's boats.

I think thunderstorms are really scary.
But they sure make great mud puddles.